Why Is There A Raisin In My Meatloaf?

by Victoria Phillips

Copyright © 2013 by Victoria Phillips
First Edition — June 2013

Illustrated by Christina Schofield

ISBN
978-1-4602-1481-7 (Paperback)
978-1-4602-1482-4 (eBook)

All rights reserved.

No part of this publication may be reproduced in any form, or by any means, electronic or mechanical, including photocopying, recording, or any information browsing, storage, or retrieval system, without permission in writing from the publisher.

Produced by:

FriesenPress

Suite 300 – 852 Fort Street
Victoria, BC, Canada V8W 1H8

www.friesenpress.com

Distributed to the trade by The Ingram Book Company

To my darling husband:

Neil, you are a wonderful caring and loving husband, father and grandfather. Our adventures together while traveling are amazing, and after all these years you still make me laugh.

Happy 60th birthday, Sweetheart

xoxo

It was Saturday, which was one of Lily's favorite days of the week. She liked Saturdays because her Daddy was home all day and didn't have to go to work. Lily was especially excited about today because Daddy said he had a big surprise for her. She wondered what the surprise might be.

"When can I have my big surprise, Daddy?" asked Lily.

Daddy smiled and said, "We will go get it right now, but we have to drive to where your surprise is."

"Yeah!" shouted Lily. She gave her mother a kiss goodbye and ran outside to get into the car.

They drove out of the city and into the country. A long time had passed and Lily was getting bored.

Then Daddy pulled into a long driveway and drove up to a house by a big red barn.

"Say hello to Mrs. Baker," said Daddy.

"Hello," said Lily shyly.

"It is nice to meet you Lily," smiled Mrs. Baker. "Your father has told me that you love puppies."

"I sure do," said Lily with a giggle.

"Well," said Daddy, "Mrs. Baker has some puppies that she wants to show you."

"There are three puppies—two girls and one boy. They are Pomeranian puppies, so they will not grow to be very big," explained Mrs. Baker.

"Oh my!" said Lily with a big smile on her face. "Can I hold one? Can I please?"

"Yes," said Daddy. "This is your surprise Lily! Mrs. Baker is looking for good loving homes for her puppies to go to. If you like one of the puppies you may keep one."

All of the puppies were so cute, but the little boy puppy kept pulling on Lily's dress, trying to play with her. When she picked him up, he licked her face and gave her lots of little kisses. He liked to be cuddled, and was so soft and fluffy.

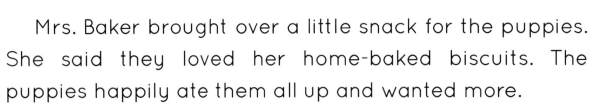

Mrs. Baker brought over a little snack for the puppies. She said they loved her home-baked biscuits. The puppies happily ate them all up and wanted more.

"Oh, Daddy," said Lily, "I want *this* one. He loves me and I love him. Can we keep him Daddy? Can we?"

"I think you picked the perfect puppy," said Daddy. "What will you call him?"

"I want to call him 'Biscuit', because he loves to eat biscuits."

"What a great name!" said Daddy with a laugh.

As Lily danced with excitement she said, "Come on Biscuit—let's go home!"

When they got home everybody played with Biscuit until it was bedtime.

Biscuit tried to sleep but was lonely in his new little bed all by himself. He began to cry.

"It's okay, Biscuit," said Lily. "You can sleep with me if you like."

So Lily picked Biscuit up and brought him up onto the bed beside her. He curled up and they fell fast asleep together.

Time passed and Biscuit was growing bigger. Soon it was time for Biscuit to go see the vet for his check-up.

The vet said Biscuit looked very happy and healthy. Then he asked Lily, "How is Biscuit doing at home?"

"He's my best friend," said Lily, "but he doesn't listen very well. He ripped up Daddy's newspaper into little pieces before Daddy got to read it."

"That sounds just like the kind of thing a puppy would do," said the vet. "You need to buy Biscuit some chew toys and you should try—"

But before the vet could say anything else, Biscuit saw a cat, and started barking. He jumped off the table to run out of the room. The poor kitty was so scared!

When they got home, the first thing Biscuit did was pick up one of Mommy's slippers in his mouth.

"No, Biscuit! Drop it!" shouted Mommy as she chased him through the living room.

Mommy had a very angry look on her face. "I love Biscuit but if Biscuit can't learn how to behave while he is inside the house he will have to stay outside!" she said while trying to catch her breath.

Lily picked Biscuit up and began to cry. Biscuit didn't understand what was wrong. He licked Lily's face to give her a kiss. Then he jumped onto the floor and began to run around in circles, chasing his tail, which made Lily laugh.

Daddy suggested that they could all go to the store after supper and buy Biscuit some chew toys—but first he had some work to do in the garage.

"Lily," called her mother. "It's Daddy's birthday today! Would you like to help me make him a surprise birthday supper while I finish making his birthday cake?"

"Yes," said Lily as she and Biscuit danced around the kitchen. "I will make Daddy the best birthday supper ever!" She giggled, then asked, "What should I make for him?"

"How about meatloaf?" said Mommy. "Daddy loves meatloaf."

"Okay," said Lily. She put on her apron and washed her hands.

"Want to help me, Biscuit?" she asked.

"Woof, woof!" barked Biscuit. He jumped up and down with excitement.

Mommy measured out all of the ingredients for Lily and put them on the counter for her. This way Lily only had to mix everything together in one big bowl.

"Oh my," said Mommy. "We have *just* enough oatmeal left to make the meatloaf. Make sure you mix everything together really well before you add the oatmeal. Remember, it is the oatmeal that helps to hold the meatloaf together," she explained.

"I won't forget," said Lily.

"When you are done and have the meatloaf in the pan I will help you put it into the oven," said Mommy. "Then you can go play while I finish making Daddy's cake."

"This will be fun, Biscuit! Are you ready?" Lily said. She put the hamburger into the big bowl, then she added the eggs and the spices. Lily did not like the smell of the onions. Then Lily added the tomato soup. Now it was time to squish it and mix it all together. This was the fun part!

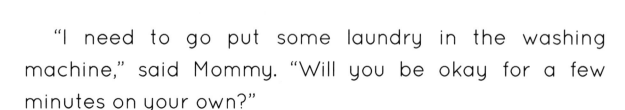

"I need to go put some laundry in the washing machine," said Mommy. "Will you be okay for a few minutes on your own?"

"Biscuit and I will be just fine," Lily answered with a giggle.

Soon Biscuit was getting bored and wanted to play. He could also smell the delicious supper Lily was making, and it was making him hungry. Biscuit started jumping up at the table, and suddenly the bowl of oatmeal tipped over and fell onto the floor. Biscuit happily started eating up all the oatmeal.

Lily cried out, "No Biscuit! Stop!" But it was too late. What was Lily to do? She remembered what her mother had said: If Biscuit did not behave, then he would have to stay outside. Lily had tears in her eyes; she didn't want Biscuit to get into any more trouble.

Lily ran to the cupboard and saw there was no oatmeal left—just like Mommy had said. But there *was* some granola cereal. *Hmm,* thought Lily. *Granola cereal is made with oatmeal. I could use this. Maybe no one will know the difference.*

"You almost ruined Daddy's birthday supper!" said Lily pointing her finger at Biscuit. "Bad boy!"

Biscuit looked sad and went and lay down under the table. He did not mean to be bad.

Lily added the granola cereal to the hamburger mix and then put it in the baking pan.

Just then Mommy came back from doing the laundry and asked Lily if everything was okay.

"Yes," said Lily. "The meatloaf is ready to go into the oven."

Lily washed up and then went to play with Biscuit.

At six o'clock Mommy called Lily and Daddy to come for supper.

When Daddy came to the dining room table to sit down, Lily shouted out "Surprise! Happy birthday, Daddy!"

"Is this for me?" said Daddy with a big smile on his face. "Thank you!"

"Biscuit and I made the meatloaf for you all by ourselves," said Lily proudly.

"Wonderful," said Daddy. "I am sure I will love it. It looks and smells delicious."

Lily watched as Daddy took his first bite to see how he liked her cooking.

Daddy said, "Mmm ... mmm ... this is delicious!" Then Daddy took a second mouthful and made a strange-looking face.

"What's the matter?" said Mommy.

"What's wrong?" said Lily.

Biscuit lay down and put his paws over his head as though he was trying to hide.

Daddy held up something between his fingers—something that he had found in his meatloaf. He looked very puzzled. Then he asked, "Why is there a raisin in my meatloaf?"

"A raisin?" said Mommy.

"Surprise!" said Lily, nervously. "Do you like it?"

"It's...ahhh...well...different," replied Daddy, looking very confused.

"Why did you put raisins in the meatloaf, Lily?" asked Mommy.

Lily told Mommy and Daddy what had happened and how she did not want Biscuit to get into trouble. She told them how she added the granola cereal to the meatloaf to replace the spilled and eaten oatmeal.

She explained how the granola cereal had oatmeal in it and how she thought it would be okay—but she had forgotten about the raisins that were also in the cereal.

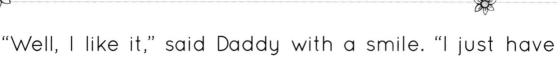

"Well, I like it," said Daddy with a smile. "I just have never had this kind of meatloaf before."

"It tastes very good," said Mommy.

Daddy laughed and said, "If it was not for Biscuit, then we would not have tried this new delicious raisin meatloaf. I think we should have Lily and Biscuit's special raisin meatloaf every year on my birthday from now on!" Daddy said as he petted Biscuit.

Everybody laughed, and Biscuit barked with excitement. Lily's raisin meatloaf was a success.

After supper, Daddy, Mommy, Lily and Biscuit all went to the pet store and bought Biscuit some chew toys.

Daddy said the chew toys were a good birthday gift for him too.

"What do you mean?" asked Lily. "I thought the toys were for Biscuit!"

"Yes, they are," said Daddy. "But now that Biscuit has some chew toys, I will be able to read my newspaper in the mornings without it being all chewed up first!"

Everybody laughed. This was a birthday everyone would remember.

THE END.

CPSIA information can be obtained
at www.ICGtesting.com
Printed in the USA
LVIC07n0425120813
347307LV00013B

9 781460 214817